SEEKER

ROLAND BYRD

SEEKER

THE NAMELESS

Publications
CYLP.co

More Books By Roland Byrd:

Sci-Fi/Fantasy Books:
A Slice of Madness

Self-Help Books:
The Law of Action
*The Prosperity Factor with Joe Vitale
Break Your Mold
Break Your Mold The Workbook
Break Your Mold Celebration and Success Journal
Reflections
The Pi of Life
Another Slice of Pi
Your Blueprint, Life by Design

Available From:
http://www.rolandbyrd.co/books-by-roland-byrd/
http://amazon.com/author/rolandbyrd

*Roland is a contributing author to this book

This book is available at special quantity discounts for bulk purchase for sales promotions, premiums, fund-raising, and educational needs. For details email Roland@RolandByrd.com.

Published by: CYL Publications: http://cylp.co

ISBN: 978-1-940324-21-0

Neither the author nor the publisher is engaged in rendering professional advice or services to the individual reader. The ideas, procedures, and suggestions contained in this book are not intended as a substitute for consulting with your physician, counselor, or therapist. All matters regarding your physical and mental health require medical supervision. Neither the author nor the publisher shall be liable or responsible for any loss or damage allegedly arising from any information or suggestions in this book.
This is a work of Transformational Fiction. First and foremost it is intended to entertain. All of the ideas in this book are the reader's responsibility to embrace or reject and as such, neither the author nor the publisher shall be liable or responsible for any loss or damage allegedly arising from any information or suggestions in this book.
By choosing to read this book, you are agreeing to the above in full.

Contents

Introduction

You're in for a wild ride!

Seeker: The Nameless is much more than a normal book. It is a work of Transformational Fiction that entertains you while simultaneously delivering positive messages directly to your unconscious mind. These messages are designed to improve your ability to cope with stressful situations, increase your sense of self-esteem, help you believe in your capabilities, and open doors to your own bright future.

Many of the passages in Seeker: The Nameless are written using Ericksonian language patterns. These patterns differ from English grammar by design. While you read Seeker: The Nameless, you'll discover subtle and positive changes in yourself as you take your own journey and evolve alongside the main character.

You can of course choose to accept the positive messages in this book or not to accept the positive messages in this book. The choice is yours.

Prepare to stretch your mind, brighten your perception of reality, and expand your spirit!

1

His hand strikes my face, sends me sprawling across the floor. I whimper. Tears well up, threaten to spill from my eyes but I blink them away. Tears are weakness and weakness is punished. That lesson I've learned well over the years. Take the pain, the anger, the hate, push them deep inside, lock them away. Deal with them later.

"Get up." He demands.

There's no question of disobedience. I stand. But not quickly enough for him. His hand lashes out again, like a coiled snake, lightning and venom exploding against the once-tender skin of my cheek. My head flies back, bounces off the wall, stars float in my vision. But somehow I manage to stay on my feet. There's that at least.

Mother looks on, helpless. Horror etched permanently in lines around her eyes. Eyes that used to laugh freely but now stare in disbelief at her inability to act, to protect her children. But she fears him too and her fear is greater than she. He's beat her down. Not physically. He saves that for us. But emotionally she's a rag doll that he stomps and bends and breaks daily. And it's taken a toll. Even the blind could see that. But still she's conflicted. Her hand twitches, an unconscious move to defend me, a subtle act of defiance, and I love her for it because I know how hard it is.

"Look at me when I'm talking to you!" He rages.

I instantly bring my eyes back to him. I've been looking at mother. Did he notice where my eyes lay? Or just that I wasn't focused on him?

He shoots a brutal glare at mother, stabs a finger at her and then at the door, "Get out of here." He growls, like a rabid dog, threats dripping from his words. She flees like a scared rabbit.

I'm sorry mother! I scream inside but cannot speak or move my eyes off him. The last thing I wanted was to get her in trouble. I won't make it worse.

He turns back to me, unbuckles his belt. It's a big, ugly thing with steel balls embedded in the leather. His favorite tool for punishment. He folds it in half, grasps both ends tightly, brings his hands together to create a six-inch gap between the sides, and then snaps them together with a crack, just like a whip.

I shudder involuntarily. He notices and smiles. "Turn around and bend over." He commands.

Even though I know what's coming, I comply. At ten, I'm much too small to fight him off. Besides, I'd rather it's this than...than...the other. That's far worse. And I always feel so dirty afterwards no matter what he says.

I turn around, grab my ankles, and grit my teeth. The whistle of his belt through the air gives me a microsecond warning before impact.

Pain! White-hot, razors and fire, it blinds me. Pain! Burning, stabbing, searing, it fills my mind, fills my being, threatens to overcome me.

He strikes repeatedly. Pulses of sheer agony, detonating, shock waves tearing through every cell of my body... Pain! Just below my bottom... Indescribable, all-encompassing, relentless... Pain! At the top of my legs, where they're most sensitive... Pain! Cutting them, exploding through my body, tearing my mind. Pain! Endless, Torment, Never Ending... Pain!

Reality fades and I drift. Formless, drifting, free...

I'm standing on a path lined with trees, pine, elm, and willow. Their trunks are close together making it impossible to see more than a few feet on either side of me. The boughs weave through each other like a tapestry of green, gold, and red. I cannot see the sun but it lights the path with a diffuse glow, like a surreal pastel painting. The path, a tunnel through the trees, disappears in the distance.

Where am I? This has never happened before and I feel wonder and fear intertwined. *Am I in heaven?*

masks the question, "Did he finally lose it, kill me this time?"

No. I feel the answer.

I turn. Look behind me. The pathway tunnels on, both sides, before me, behind me, identical. But that way, the path behind, feels...Darker. So I choose, turn back and step forward, away from the darkness and into the unknown.

Then it fades...

∞

I come back. My legs ache worse than last time, not as bad as the time before. With the exception of my dream—*Was it a dream?* I remember nothing past the sixth strike. Another memory gap. I wonder how much of my life I'll lose to this man that my mother married and once manipulated me into calling dad. I wonder how long these bruises will stain my legs, how long I'll have to keep my legs hidden at school. But it doesn't matter. I'll do it. I always do. Because my mother loves him. Because it's all I know.

It's all I know... So I keep the secrets and endure. I always do...

2

We're in the mountains. Mother's off in the cabin. I'm with Him. Him and his gun, and my Brother. And His Gun... Walking along the mountainside. Spring flowers paint the ground with gold and purple and red. The air smells sweet, and green, like pine trees and sap. Sun shines down, promising hope, lying to me. Just like it does every day. Teasing my heart and mind with threads of hope. But they're weak, fragile and they snap all too easily when He's around.

A small grey rabbit scurries across the path, stops and sniffs the air. It looks at us quizzically. As if wondering, *Who are these imposters?*

"Watch this." He whispers, the excitement obvious in his voice.

Oh no! The Gun. It's in His hand, a .44 Magnum. Big Gun. Really Big Gun. He levels it at the innocent rabbit. I can't watch... I have to. He said to. I can't, don't want to, have to... The trigger clicks back, shifts, hesitates, falls.

BOOM! Shatters the stillness, the beauty...shocks the mountainside. And the rabbit, it's gone. Vanished in a pink puff of fur, and blood, and bone, and thunder. Like a magic trick except for the gore. And just like that, an innocent life is wasted.

He turns to me and my Brother and asks, "Wasn't that cool?"

We glance at each other, my Brother and I. Silent understanding passes between us, "Yeah, great!" I lie, afraid to tell him the truth.

My Brother lies his answer too, "Awesome!"

I decide I'm a coward. Strong people stand up for themselves and what they believe, no matter how big their opponent...Cowards lie to keep from getting hurt. I stack that inside with my other labels, weakling, stupid, ugly, unlovable, timid, guilty, broken... There are many more. I can't remember when I started accepting them, my labels, but already I believe them and they come to me when I need them, like something inside knows exactly how bad I need to feel and brings me the right label...

∞

That night I dream. I'm in the cabin alone. A pack of wolves howl outside. They scratch at the walls, pound the windows, bite through the wood. The wolves smell me, they see me, they're ravenous.

I huddle in the middle of the room, like a helpless rabbit staring down the barrel of a .44. The wolves tear the walls with their teeth, the holes growing larger every moment. They force their heads through the holes, red eyes blazing, snarling, seeking me with their teeth. They cannot reach me, not yet. In a macabre dance they pull their heads back and tear at the walls more, like synchronized killing machines.

One forces his head through, rams the wall, and widens the gap. A board snaps. He's through, lunging at my throat...

∞

I'm in the tunnel again. The sun sits higher in the sky. I've been walking, I know because my feet are sore and that's okay. Better sore feet than the alternative. But what *is* the alternative. I'm uncertain now drifting deeply inside...relaxing as I walk deeper into the tunnel.

And I walk, deeper, and deeper, into the tunnel and my cares drift away like smoke on the wind. Ahead, there's an opening in the side, like a doorway in the trees. I walk to it, step through. I don't know why I know but it's the right thing to do.

A bowl shaped clearing greets me. Birds chirp and sing. A small rabbit darts across, a grey streak, smarter than the one today. My eyes drift to the middle of the open space, are drawn there as if pulled by an invisible string. A lone tree sags against itself, like it's trying to fold in half from both sides simultaneously and the absurdity of the action keeps it upright. The bark is like weathered skin, brown, leathery, and wrinkled from too much sun. Its branches droop, heavy with age, brushing the ground in some places. But the leaves... Oh the leaves are brilliant with rainbow hues glowing like a thousand fires in the sunlight.

"Who goes there?" A voice rasps through the silence.

I stare at the tree. Did it speak? Is it possible?

"Don't just stand there." The voice cuts the silence again, "Come over here where I can see you."

The sound seems to come from the tree but there's no evidence of it speaking. I investigate, step around the trunk, and see a man, with skin so old and weathered it matches the tree's bark, sitting against the trunk. His head turns and he looks right at me. But he cannot see me, his eyes are solid white, like marbles, white like the wisps of hair above his temples and on his chin.

"So... It is you." He voice, though rough and gravely, smiles in time with his mouth.

"Me?" I ask stupidly.

"Yes. You." He points right at my heart. "I've been waiting for you these long, long years. A lifetime, wait-

ing. Sitting here with this tree, as my only companion."
He pats the trunk beside him and chuckles.

"But... But how do you know who I am? When you..."
I trail off, uncertain whether mentioning his blindness is
taboo.

"When I'm blind?" He smiles again. "Yes. I'm blind,"
He slaps his hand over his eyes, "but I can see more than
you I think." And he laughs.

Uncertain what to think or say, I mumble, "But...
why? Why are you waiting for me?" *I'm nobody, worthless..*, the voice in my head finishes the thought.

His head moves forward, juts toward me a fraction.
His eyes squint slightly, wrinkling more. I didn't think
that was possible but it is. I swear he's staring right
through me. Staring hard, like he's examining my soul. I
stand still, deer in the headlights, afraid to move. Fear...
such a big part of my life. Fear and sadness...my true
companions. At least they'll never desert me. Not like...
Father.

The old man sits back and nods, smiles again, and
says, "Yes. *It is you!* You are somebody and somebody
is you and you are the one I've been waiting for..." He
chuckles again.

I'm stunned and confused. "But, you never answered
my question." The words leap from my mouth uninvited
and hang in the air.

"Your question?" He cocks his head to the side. If I wasn't so frustrated I'd laugh. He reminds me of an old dog, waiting for scraps at the table.

I groan inwardly, then repeat myself, "Why are you waiting for me?" I don't know why, but discovering the answer feels urgent, like my life hangs in the balance.

"Isn't it obvious? To help you on your quest!" He gestures to the side, toward something in the distance.

"My...Quest?" I search my mind for reasons I'd go on a quest, find none. "What quest?"

He shakes his head, as if dealing with a stubborn child. Then says, "Your quest to discover your true name."

"But I already know my name!" I shout, anger, fear, and sadness boiling inside me, threatening to surface. I open my mouth to speak and he cuts me off.

"Do you?" He arches an eyebrow and leans closer.

And I discover my mind is blank. I cannot find my name. When I seek it, labels given to me by others swarm through my head. A sound escapes my lips, "Coward..." Is that my name?

The old man exhales forcefully, "No!" Then he softens, "Coward is a mere label. An idea placed in your unconscious mind by cruel people who would hurt you rather than face their own inadequacies. You are lost, confused by life, unaware of the power of your mind, of your heart, so you took the label and made it your own. *Release it...Now! Release all the labels Now!*"

I feel a subtle shift inside, a tingle down my spine, like my brain is rewiring itself. "Then who am I?" I plead.

"You are the Nameless."

"Nameless?" I repeat.

He nods again, "Yes. Your true name is hidden. Discover it and you *discover your power!*"

∞

I wake, shake the sleep from my head. *What a dream*, I muse. *What a weird dream.* But still... Something feels different, as if a new future awaits.

3

Father's back. For five years he was gone. Vanished. I used to think he was dead. He took us, me and Brother, to a church once where they had a laser-light show and played rock music on a stage. It was bizarre to me. Then, around the time Father went MIA, I heard about a cult of people who all drank poisoned juice in a park and died. Men, women, children... all dead from drinking the juice. So I figured it was the same church and he was dead. It was the only thing that made sense to me, the only reason I could comprehend why he would disappear from my life. The only reason why he wouldn't rescue me from Him...

But he wasn't dead and he's back and I'm angry with him. So very angry. My fury churns beneath the surface threatening to explode. Like a famous movie character once said, "I'm always angry." Just before he turned into the hero and saved the day. But it doesn't help me, not like that. It gets me in trouble and sometimes it hurts others, words are sharp, like razors. And razors cut deeper than fists. I learned that the hard way too.

But I can't be angry with Father. So I shove it inside, bury it deep with all the rest. I imagine my anger is stored in a nuclear waste dump. But those cans decay and it seeps out from time to time, despite my best efforts.

And now Father is back. And he's getting married to someone I've never met. Brother and I are going to be there, for the wedding. The first time I see Father in over five years and it's when he decides to get married.

Oh Joy! I can barely contain myself.

And Mother is acting strange too. For her, Father coming back into our lives seems a bad thing. But at least Mother's husband hasn't beat me or Brother for a while. I guess it wouldn't do to have us all marked up at Father's wedding. So, there's that at least...

On the plane, acceleration pushes me deep into my seat and I imagine I'm on a rocket, leaving earth behind for good. Leaving my worries and my pain and my old life behind. Starting over...

∞

And I find myself back on the path, in the trees. It's dark, near pitch black in the surrounding forest. Torches, held securely to the trees by wrought iron brackets, line the sides of the tunnel. Firelight flickers, dancing on the ground, swaying through the tree trunks. I hadn't noticed the torches before but I hadn't been looking either. Funny how that works, something can be right there, right in front of you, but until you're ready to see it, it might as well not exist.

I look for the opening in the wall, I want to speak to the old man again. But I cannot find it. And deep inside I know that's somewhere behind me, in the past, where it belongs and where it must stay. The old man gave me what he needed to and we both moved on.

I walk on, each step carrying me deeper and deeper along the path, deeper into the unknown. *Why do I keep coming here?* It doesn't happen very often. Sometimes I think this is a dream, a fantasy to keep me sane...

Ha! That's a joke. Me...sane. I'm fairly certain I left that state a long time ago in my quest to survive. I escape reality at every chance, movies, books, cartoons, anything I can find to distract me from the truth...

I hear music and laughter in the distance. Without knowing why, I run. Faster, faster, toward the sounds. Then flickering lights appear through the trunks to my left and without thinking why, I leave the trail. Carefully, picking my way through the undergrowth and darkness I move closer, closer... Until I see them.

I stop and watch, afraid they'll vanish too, like Father did.

They're all wearing masks and dancing around a bonfire. The scent of roasted food fills my nostrils, reminds me I'm hungry. One of them, a woman wearing a goat mask, spots me and walks over.

"And who might you be?" She grasps my wrist in a surprisingly strong grip and gently pulls me into the clearing.

"I'm...I'm..." I realize I've lost my name again but then I remember what the old man told me and say, "I'm Nameless."

Her face lights with a smile, "How wonderful! We've been waiting for you." She winks, then clasps her hands before her breast and calls to the others, "The Nameless is here! The Nameless is here!" She turns back to me, says, "Now we can begin!" And pulls me into the dance.

We dance for a time. A raucous tune carrying our feet. Once the fire has burnt low, we sit and eat. I feel something I'd forgotten...Peace. It radiates from deep within me, a place deeper than the anger, deeper than the pain. I realize I've buried peace too and it's longing to emerge, to heal me.

The goat mask woman sits next to me. She reaches into the fire with tongs, grabs a glowing ember, and holds it out to me, "Take it." She commands.

"No!" I shriek, my hands instinctively going to my lap for protection.

She tilts her head, much like the old man once did, and asks, "Why not?" Still holding the coal, darker on the outside now from exposure to the air but still blistering hot, for me to take.

"Because it'll burn me!" I answer.

"So?" She says and shakes the tongs urgently above my lap.

"Wh...why would I hold onto something that's going to hurt me?" I scoot backward off my seat and stare at her in disbelief.

She smiles. "Why indeed... Why indeed...." She says and winks.

∞

The lurch of the plane and bark of rubber tires jolt me back to reality as the plane lands. I feel odd... And we're here and father is waiting...

4

The wedding's over. It wasn't so bad. And it was good to see Father again, if only for a week.

We're living with Grandmother now. Mother and Him have managed to get us kicked out of yet another rental home. So Grandmother came to the rescue. Again...

It's been a long day. I'm tired. My bunk, the top one, feels good. I relax, start to drift off... So tired. Then, in the darkness a hand, a big hand, rough with callouses, clasps over my mouth, my nose. I can't breathe. The hand realizes this and loosens slightly.

"Shhhh..." The dark voice whispers in my ear. A weight, so heavy, so vile, climbs on top of me...

∞

I'm back on the path. It's daytime now. The sun glows through the trees. But it's cold, so cold. The leaves are gone. I can see the sky, it's grey...grey like my heart, through the canopy of tangled branches. Mist trails upward, drifting from my mouth in time with my breath. I'm glad to be here. So glad, here instead of...

I look up and spin, arms open. The path blurs, a kaleidoscope of grey, brown, and pale sky. I spin until I fall down, dizzy. The world cavorts, looping before my eyes. I laugh and my heart opens a little, not much, just a crack.

When my head stops spinning I stand. I look before me, behind me.

Great!

I'm not sure which way to go. I don't know what's before and what's behind... The sun is directly overhead... but which way is it going? If I knew that I could find my compass points. Then I realize that compass points won't help because I've never known which way I traveled, here in this place. So I close my eyes and stand still, like a statue, listening, feeling, just being.

After a time it comes to me, a vision. I turn around and walk. And walk. For hours it seems. The sun has moved, down to my right as the day wanes. South it is. I'm walking south and I choose to remember that because it might matter and it's good to remember things that matter. Shadows stretch right to left across the path before me, weaving a pattern of light and shadow on the ground and through the trees. It's reminiscent of a painting I saw once, a Native American Brave and his palomino horse are hidden, camouflaged in the forest.

And I walk on.

Dusk is falling. I'm relaxed, so relaxed as I walk deeper, ever deeper into my dreamscape. And I wonder if it's a dream. But how can it be anything else? And it's so real. So I wonder... In most dreams I feel the dream, like a veneer of illusion coating my awareness. This is different. It's crisp, solid, cold. There are no unexplained jumps from one place to the next...Except for appearing here I guess, and shrug.

Then I see it. In the distance the tunnel splits into three paths, like a trident. It's my vision come to life.

As I approach a voice, light like spring mist but oddly halting, hails me, "Who... approaches... the crossroads?"

This wasn't in my vision though, that ended where the tunnel split. I figure I only needed to know enough to find it, the crossroads. The rest is up to me. I'm less than ten feet from the junction. I stop, open my mouth to answer and grimace. It shouldn't be a surprise that I cannot find my name. But it is. I answer, "I am The Nameless." I've never used it as a title before. I like how it feels.

Whispers, then hurried rustling, three children, young, perhaps 4 years old, hop onto the path. One stands before each choice of pathway. "We're glad you're here!" The one on the left says. "We've been waiting for you a very long time." The one in the middle says. "For most of our lives." The one on the right says.

"Why am I not surprised?" I mumble bemused. They frown, look at each other. After a moment they shrug, eerily synchronized, and look back at me... Waiting. For what, though. For what?

Silence. It encompasses us, like a soft blanket woven from the fleece of knowing and not knowing and wisdom and doubt. It's good for now. And when it's not my unconscious nudges me and I ask, "Why are you waiting for me?"

"But..." The left one says. "We're not..." The middle one says. "Anymore..." The right one says. And they shrug again.

I sigh, shake my head, and ask, "Why *were* you waiting for me?"

They lean close to each other, heads touching, and whisper excitedly. After a time, they go back to their places and their eyes and mouths crinkle in joy. "So we..." The left one says. "Can answer..." The center one says. "Your questions!" The right one says.

"Do you have to talk that way?" I ask in exasperation.

"How else..." The left one says. "Would we..." The middle one says. "Ever talk?" The right one finishes.

It's my turn to shrug, so I do. Then I gently massage my temples. "So... Which path should I take?" I ask.

"We cannot..." The left one says. "Control..." The middle one says. "Others..." The right one says.

"We cannot..." The left one says. "Control..." The middle one says. "Events..." The right one says.

"But we can..." The left one says. "Always control..." The middle one says. "Our choices..." The right one says.

"And no one..." The left one says. "Can ever take..." The middle one says. "That power from you." The right one finishes.

I take this in and let it swirl in my soul as I look from path to path, uncertain. I close my eyes and wait but nothing comes to me. I'm blank, a void, nameless. So I open my eyes and ask, "How do I know which path to choose?"

"What do..." The left one says. "You desire..." The middle one says. "From life..?" The right one says.

What do I desire from life? I'd never considered that before. The question is strange to me, like new shoes that don't fit quite right. But I know that, if I wear it long enough, it will mold itself to me or perhaps I'll mold myself to it. I'm uncertain but I try it on anyway. And in time it does, fit me that is. I know because the answer springs unbidden to mind and leaps from my mouth, "I want to be the best person I can be and to help others have better lives!"

"Despite what you've gone through..." The left one says. "You're certain that this..." The middle one says. "Is what you want..?" The right one says.

"Most would choose revenge..." The left one says and points behind itself. "Or escape from pain..." The middle one says and points behind itself. And the right one remains silent but cocks its head inquisitively as if asking me to affirm my choice.

"Yes." I say without hesitation, "I want to be the best person I can be and to help others have better lives!" And I feel warmth and truth spread through my being, encompassing me in peace as I see this truth. Only now peace feels like the old friend I knew it was but had merely forgotten.

"Then let us integrate..." The left one says and steps to the middle leaving its path open. "And serve your..." The middle one says and the two step to the right leaving the middle path open as well. "Higher purpose..." The right one says and they clasp hands. As their hands touch their bodies start to quiver, and blur, and merge until there is only one.

The single child looks at me and says, "You've made a wise choice. Are you certain it's the right choice for you?"

"Yes." I reply, at peace.

The child waves its hand in the direction of the two abandoned paths and they vanish, as if they never existed. Then it turns to me, "Everything is choice. Every moment is choice. And everything you choose sets the path of your life. This is your power. None can take it from you. Use it well." Then it bows deeply and steps from the path, beckoning me to continue.

And I do. I step on the new path...

∞

It's morning and there's another gap in my memory. The night before is gone, vanished like the two paths I choose to leave behind. And I realize it doesn't matter. He can hurt me physically. He can use me... But he can never take away my power to choose my path. I'm small on the outside. Only eleven. I'm smaller by far than him physically. But I'm a Giant inside and he cannot take that away unless I let him.

And I'm done letting him. My decision is made, in stone. I'll endure what I must while I must. But the joke's on Him because instead of letting Him crush me I'll take His evil and use it for good. I'll use these things to grow, to learn how to alleviate others' suffering, to make the world a better place. That's my choice to make and I make it Now...

5

'm hiding in a closet. It's my birthday...and I'm hiding in a closet. Father told me to, said we're running away to Canada so I won't have to go back. I'm living with Father and his wife. I went to visit and said I didn't want to go back. So they told me I could stay. But Mother, though she'd told me in the past I could choose...proved it a lie and said I had to come back. But I didn't want to come back and I don't want to go back and so the war began.

And there are lawyers and now the cops and now I'm hiding in a closet...on my birthday. Waiting to run away to Canada with Father. There's a knock on the closet door and Father opens it, and he leans in, and he says, "You have to go back. I'm sorry. We'll continue fighting them... But for now you have to go back." And I realize the war is over and I've lost and a hole gapes open in my heart, a black pit of betrayal and despair that swallows me whole and may never heal.

Father takes me to the police station, leads me inside, and I see them, Mother and Him... Waiting. He smiles, an evil thing that vanishes before anyone else sees it. I die inside and feel my inner Giant hang its head in sorrow and shrink and shrink and shrink...until it's small and powerless, like me.

And I'm in the car and we're driving home... But it's not my home. I haven't got one. I'm going to hell. On my birthday, being dragged to hell by those who say they only want what's best for me but who really only care about their selfish desires. And I want to die, for real, to end the pain. If I'm going to hell I might as well go to the real one. It can't be worse than this. But I can't end my life because I don't know how. And because they're watching. And because I'm afraid...

∞

And I'm on the path. But it's different this time. The forest is gone, burnt to the ground. All around me...desolation. Withered tree stumps, black skeletons, lifeless and charred like my heart, march mile after mile after mile to the horizon. And for the first time here, I cry. I fall to the ground and sob uncontrollably until my eyes are swollen and sore and my throat is raw and then I remember what happens to me when I cry. He hits me more. Crying is weakness and weakness isn't tolerated.

When I cry, He hits me harder and harder until I stop. I haven't cried in years...until now.

But He can't reach me here. I'm safe. It's my refuge and now it's desolation...death and destruction everywhere I look. And even so, I'm safe here. He can't hurt me here. He can't touch me here. Safe.

I know it deeply and feel my tears dry and I wipe my face and I stand back up. I look around. In the distance I see a shape, lying in the middle of bleakness. I walk toward it cautiously at first, then faster and faster, I'm drawn to it, compelled. Something pulls at me until I sprint the last bit. And now I'm standing near it. Not close enough to touch but close enough to see.

It's strange, this creature. It seems human, but its smoke-blackened skin and the way it lays, in a tight ball, the fetal position, makes it hard to know. I step closer, closer...

It doesn't move as I approach. *Is it alive?* I wonder. It must have escaped the fire because no burn marks mar its skin. I take a final step. I'm right behind it, my shin almost touching its back. I reach out and touch it, gently shake it by the shoulder.

It groans but doesn't move.

"Are you okay?" I ask.

"No!" It says in a familiar voice that I know I should be able to place but can't.

I kneel next to it but stay behind its back. Something inside tells me that it must be the one to reveal itself. So I ask, "What happened?" And I wait.

It groans and twitches and...seems to grow an inch or two and says, "You Gave Up!" And it turns to face me and it is me but it's not me... It's my Giant, only small now. But not as small as it was a moment ago.

I ponder, turn my eyes inside and look at my soul. I take it out and study it. It's damaged, true, but not as badly as I'd imagined. *Interesting*, I think and look back at my Giant. It's grown more, only a little, and I say, "You're right. I did. I'm sorry..."

My Giant sits up, stares at me with hard eyes, like they're chiseled from stone, accusing eyes, like this is all my fault. And I think Fault...such a horrid word, implying that someone is completely and utterly to blame... And I am, to blame, at fault for this.

"You're doing it again! Stop It!" My Giant shoves me. Not so hard to knock me down, just hard enough to get my attention.

I pry my eyes away from my soul and look at my Giant. It's smaller again. Not as small as it was when I found it, but still...smaller than a moment ago. "What happened?" I ask and sit on soot coated earth.

It scowls at me, its face full of disgust, "You keep forgetting!" It turns away, shakes its head, turns back and screams, "WHAT HAPPENED TO YOU?" It throws its arms in the air, then stabs its finger at my face, YOU"RE STRONGER THAN THIS!"

I recoil and skitter backward like a scared insect. Then it hits me, lays me flat, and I stop moving. What did my Giant say? Strong..? Me...Strong? I immediately reject the idea even though it tingles with truth, "I'm not strong." I shake my head and watch my Giant shrink an inch before my eyes.

My Giant rolls its eyes. They're softer now, the hard edges gone, its eyes peering into me, like it's searching for something. "Yes, you are...Strong. Stronger than you know." It says and then offers its hand.

I take it. It pulls me to my feet. I'm taller than my Giant now. Funny, that one. I chuckle. My Giant grows an inch. I feel its hand shift slightly in mine. I frown at it. It starts walking, still holding my hand, pulling me along.

"Have you ever stopped to consider the things you've overcome?" My Giant asks, casually, like it's asking the time or inquiring about the weather.

I search my mind, come up empty, and reveal this truth, "No." I shrug. Strong was never a word I'd attached to myself in any form. I'd never contemplated it or even wondered about it. It's alien to me.

My Giant stops, takes my face in its hands, and looks me in the eyes. "Who learned to choose your path despite the choices of others?"

I don't answer out loud but a tiny voice in my head says, *I did*. And I feel a small brush of pride against my heart. My Giant grows a little before my eyes.

"Who learned to let go of things that are hurting you?" My Giant lifts an eyebrow inquiringly.

This time I manage to force out a single word, "M...M...Me." I stammer. Feeling something strange stirring in my bosom. My Giant grows larger, it's bigger than me now, not by much, but bigger still.

"Who discovered that your true path is helping others?"

I smile slightly and say, "I... D...did. I did." And my Giant grows larger, its hands are now twice the size of mine and it has to stoop nearly double to look me in the eyes.

"And who had the courage to say you wanted to live with Father?" My Giant smiles and slaps me on the shoulder like an old friend.

"I did." I say without hesitation and then frown, "But they took it away..." I purse my lips and sigh, "They took me away." I realize it doesn't feel as devastating now as it did only a moment ago. *I wonder why?*

"Because you're remembering how strong you are." My Giant answers and grows again...

∞

And I'm in the car. Huddled on the floorboards behind the front seat as we drive through the night, down, down the freeway through the black night... But it's going to be okay. I know that now. Somehow I'll survive and grow even stronger for it...

6

They're fighting again. Brother and I huddle in a corner, being as small, as quiet as possible. After all, it's our fault. He tells us that every time they fight now, that it's our fault. And he takes it out on us when she's not around or not looking or too exhausted to know what's going on... Which is a lot of the time. And we are why they fight, partly, because Mother has started telling Him to leave us alone. And alone He leaves us when she knows, when she's there, but she's not there... Most of the time.

And He's screaming at her, right in her face like a rabid wolf, jaws snapping, salvia flying, howling at her. Mother stands her ground. She's like the badger, small, fierce, unwilling to back down regardless the size of her foe. I'm proud of her for that. I love her for that because despite her weakness and the pain Brother and I've endured, and the pain she's endured, she's fighting back.

He's never hit Mother. He has some unwritten rule where it's okay for Him to hurt children, to hurt Brother and me, but not to hurt adults, like brother and I are worth less because we're smaller, like the value of life is measured by how tall you are... And I think of my Giant and I smile, a quick little smile that vanishes as fast as it appears. I'm bigger than Him, at least inside...where it really counts.

But he is angry. So angry. He is rage. If there were a god of rage it would be Him. And He storms over and picks up the present Mother bought Him, when things were fresh and His many masks still covered His true self. The delicate covered wagon model. Mother scrimped and saved for the wagon. She was so proud of it, a true gift of love and sacrifice. And he smashes it, throws it against the ground with all His power. It disintegrates, like the grey rabbit, except this time the carnage is Mother's heart. I see it in her face. The mask of anger falls off and she looks like a little girl, sad, lonely, lost...broken... Broken because she still loves him. Despite everything He's done, everything He's put her through, despite everything, she still loves him. And He's just shattered her heart. I see it. I wonder if He sees it.

And then I know he does because there is silence and His face is pale, like a dead person's, pale and scared. "I'm sorry..." He says and reaches toward Mother. But she shakes her head, steps away. Her whole body trembles and heaves with her sadness and she flees the room.

He stands there, like a small child...diminished, looking confused, like something's missing and He doesn't know what it is or where to find it. Then he sees us, brother and I, and the color floods back into his face and he screams, "THIS IS ALL YOUR FAULT!" And he lunges toward us.

And I feel a new emotion for Him, one that I never thought I could. I feel pity...

∞

I'm lying on the ground. Birds chirp and sing and sunlight warms my face like a gentle song of hope. I open my eyes. A huge foot sits, mingled with grass and flowers, next to my face. I look up, smile. It's my Giant. It sees me and smiles back.

Neither of us speak, not yet. The time isn't now for that. Time... It passes strangely here, if it passes at all. But it must, pass that is, I'm in the middle of what was the desolation. Now saplings dot the landscape, nestled among the burnt husks of the old forest like children clinging to their mothers' skirts. And the ground is coated with grass and flowers as if Nature herself pulled up a blanket and tucked the saplings in.

I look back up, up, up at my Giant. Its head is as big as my body, its torso as big as a house. And I wonder what I've done to help it grow and I've no answer.

But sometimes answers aren't necessary when healing. Sometimes healing just is, and it happens, healing does happen...Now. And I don't have to know why, I only have to accept it, the healing, my healing, Now...accept it. And I do and I feel the healing move through me like clean water flowing through a mountain brook and I shudder in joy.

And now it's time. So I break the silence, "Why am I here... Instead of on the path?"

My Giant looks down on me and smiles, "Some journeys have a destination without a clear path..." Its voice rumbles like a slow landslide down its body to my ears and it points to a distant spot, a mountain, grim, foreboding, taller than its peers with snow crusting its upper reaches and peak lost in clouds. Clouds, dark and swirling, full of lightning, a tempest, bathing the mountain in chaos.

My Giant opens its mouth again and more words come rolling down, "Sometimes, the path matters less than the destination. Sometimes the path is the destination. For you, now, this is the first." And my Giant stands, smiles again, and begins to walk away

"Wait!" I call, frantic, uncertain what to do. My Giant stops, turns, waits. I go on, "What will I find there? What do I do?"

"Beyond the mountain, stands a lonely Castle. The Castle time forgot. It knows you and you will know it but first you must go...because it waits..." Then my Giant turns and walks away and I marvel at its size and strength and courage. And I wonder...

So I stand, breathe deep, stretch, and survey the mountain. It's vast, larger than all its neighbors, but I cannot tell its true size because I have no sense of its scale. Is it ten miles, thirty, one-hundred miles distant? I've no idea. Then I realize it doesn't matter how far away it is or how large it is or how difficult my path, because my journey began the day I was born. And this is simply the next phase.

A smile shines on my face, hope burns in my heart, and I begin...

∞

The room is dark. Brother is sleeping. I hear his breath, slow, steady, deep. The kind of sleep that masks pain, that paints your mind with dreams, that makes you feel, if only a moment, feel like everything's going to be alright.

I listen for Him, for Mother. Nothing. Nothing but silence and brother's breathing and the ticking of the clock on the wall. All the anger and hate and rage have been put to bed. And I'm tired, so tired. But it's different this time because I've forgotten how to hate or hate has forgotten me... I'm uncertain which. All I know is that I'm tired and I feel peaceful and I know my meaning and my meaning knows me and it's more powerful than I'd ever imagined...before.

I close my eyes on the darkness. A vision of my Giant, smiling down, greets me, and I fade away...

7

The wind howls. I can barely stand and I love it. I imagine I'm a kite and the wind lifts me up and I sail away, into the sky, drifting, drifting into heaven. And I realize I'm dreaming and I don't care, so I go back to the dream and I sail on the wind, away on the wind, far away to the land of hope and light, where animals speak and laughter sings on the wind. The wind carries me, drifting, drifting, drifting to the edge of the sea where love paints the sky and courage lifts the sun...

And I wake and sigh. Mother mopes around, dead inside, loveless and lost. It's so hard to watch, her pain, her loss, and to feel it mingled with my joy, to feel it's because of me that He is leaving, after all He told me so, that it was all my fault. And maybe it is, all my fault, but try as I might, I cannot feel sorrow at His passing...out of our lives. Mother and Him are divorcing and I dance inside and still it's hard to witness her pain.

And then she pulls me aside and says, "I'm sending you to live with Father." And I stagger back, shock tingling through me. This is what I wanted but it's not what I want. He is leaving...and now I'm leaving too?

Why Mother, oh why did you fight so hard to bring me back if only to let me go these few months later? Are brother and I merely pawns that you cast aside once you won the war? Have we fulfilled our purpose? Am I nothing to you but a trophy and now a symbol of your loss to banish from your sight?

And I run away and hide, conflicted, wanting to feel happy that I'm going to live with Father, wanting to feel that Mother loves me enough to make me stay, to ask me to stay, to give me the choice, at least...the choice...

∞

The mountain is nearer now, the saplings taller, animals frolic in pools of spring sunshine spilling over and down between clouds, white as snow in the sky. Yes, the mountain is nearer and it's so very far away. I'd no idea its vastness. Nothing prepared me for this. Its base was hidden by horizon's curve when last I saw it.

But now I know, oh yes, I know. Its gentle slopes bleed gently into the prairie for miles and miles...and miles. And its peak hides in the clouds, under blankets of snow and ice, the kind that never melts, and its neighbors are half its height... And I must climb it. My Giant said so. Climb it and go over it and find The Castle that time forgot... The Castle that's waiting for me and that knows me and that I will know too. And it feels impossible and I must do it and I know I can do it because someone once told me in the future or the past or a timeless place, I cannot remember where or when, they told me, "It's good you can do hard things." And it is. And I know it. Hard, it is. Difficult, yes. Impossible, perhaps. Call it what you will... Regardless, this mountain is mine and I will climb it...

8

rother and I ride our bikes through the field. We jump and we skid and we race and he wins and I win. Our legs pump furiously and our lungs heave like billows feeding the fires of bliss as we tear through weeds and grass and dirt, clouds of dust chasing us, chasing but never catching because we're faster than the wind.

And movement wipes away sadness and I forget the reasons I feel less than because the reasons are all illusions held within my mind, illusions released by action, by activity, by existing in this moment, this eternal now of joy. I realize, as the tires spin so fast they buzz like hungry bees, Brother is my one true friend, the one who's always been there no matter what, the one who's never abandoned me...Brother. And I love him all the more for it.

∞

Chapter 8

I wake in the dirt, in this place, with the ground beneath me and the sky above. Sky of black, a velvet curtain hung with diamonds sparkling like tiny dots of hope in the darkness. And as the mist of my breath curls up from my lips, crosses the path of the moon, I wonder why my name matters?

What's in my name that I cannot remember it here? I remember it there, in that place, in the other...and I wonder if that name is my true name or if it's just letters strung together like random bits of dust. And it comes to me that I'm uncertain what's real. When I'm here, in this place, this is real. I see, feel, hear, think, exist with all the clarity of reality. And when I'm there I do the same but I'm not the same here and there are subtle differences in me. There I'm trapped in my mind by the thoughts and the past and the fears of the future but here I'm The Nameless, wandering...wandering but not lost, seeking the truth of me that somehow is kept secret by the name I've lost. But to lose something you must first have it and I've never had my name here, so did I really lose it or is it waiting to find me when I've earned the right to know who I am..?

And with these thoughts spinning through the ether of my mind I roll over and let darkness sweep over me with the warmth of forgetting...

9

I'm with a friend in the mountains outside of town and we're hanging out and camping and drinking...which I rarely do because I hate the way alcohol takes away my control and my reason...but I'm doing now because I hate the pain inside more than I hate alcohol.

And I've had too much, far too much to drink. And my head is cloudy and my thoughts are swirling like puffs of black smoke in the wind. I'm staggering and swearing and playing around the fire, dancing around the edges like a child dancing around a mud puddle when parents are watching. And I see the chain I brought, a big chain, the kind they use to lock the gates at abandoned factories, and I cannot remember why I brought it...but brought it I did and why doesn't matter when my thoughts are smoke. So I see it and grab it and lay it in the fire, in the hottest part, because that's the best thing to do with a chain when you're camping and drunk and playing with fire...

Night casts its cloak over me, over the world, and the moon comes out and winks stars into the sky. And my chain grows hotter, hotter, hotter until it's glowing red and I love it. I love my chain, it keeps me bound in the familiar darkness of the night, my night inside where the pain and darkness churn in their ocean of eternal night. And the chain grows hotter, hotter, hotter, but the part I left out of the fire is cool so I pick it up and I feel the heat radiating against my legs and it's good. And I take the chain and swing it, a glowing red circle of fire in the night, like a shield of flame protecting me, making me invincible. And I see a tree, old, lonely, broken, and I go to it and swing my chain attacking a time-worn branch. And I miss.

The chain whips down, around, whistles next to my face, singes my hair, and wraps around my forearm and wrist like an angry boa constrictor.

It sears my flesh and I scream and I hear the sizzle of my skin and smell the burning and I shake my arm frantically and the chain peels off, falls to the ground taking bits of me with it. And it hurts and I'm drunk so it doesn't hurt as badly as it could. My arm throbs, like a giant blood-pressure cuff is squeezing it, releasing it, squeezing it again...

∞

Chapter 9

The Mountain looms nearer, hanging over me like an ancient god, filling my heart, my soul, my mind with its power and every day brings me closer to the start. The start of what..? I cannot say but I know it's the start of something, something I'll chose when the time to choose comes.

And I walk and I walk and the days turn to night and reality bends me to its will or it to my will...I am uncertain which is the reality or is there really "the reality"...and I realize that reality is what it is because I make it so. I make it what I want...right? And I wonder why I choose the reality where I'm sick and wounded and frail when I can just as easily and effortlessly *choose the reality where I'm strong and whole and vibrant...* where I understand that *my choices make me* and then influence me to make more of the same choices that reinforce themselves and justify themselves and make perfect sense to me as they create the cycle of thought and action and perception and focus that is me.

And the me that is the me that I've chosen to be walks toward the mountain looming over me and wonders why I keep falling down when *I can easily stand* and why I feel pain when *I can effortlessly feel joy*? *Joy is in me, joy is me* buried under pain and thought and cycles of despair...but it's there. I know it is because I feel it, feel joy tugging at my heart when I forget to feel the sadness that I've chosen, when I *remember to forget depression* or *forget to remember depression* I'm never certain which but I know the choice is mine and I make it Now.

And I remember to remember to think of the happy things, the good things, the positive things in every situation because they're always there when I look for them Now because everything is balance and if there is negative then there is positive and I must seek it to find it because I find what I seek.

So I wonder what am I seeking...?

And I wake in the night with stars dotting the heavens like a million, million fireflies, and the Milky Way flowing like a river across the sky... And I'm sweating and I'm cold and my stomach is knotted, threatening to heave itself from my body, and my thoughts are still puffs of black smoke and the world swirls around me, a kaleidoscope of nauseating sensation and I close my eyes and hope I survive because I realize I have alcohol poisoning and I'm dehydrated and my friend is asleep and no one can help me because I can't move or speak or help myself...and I wish this night would end.

10

I'm sad and alone and sad... And the tears flow like rivers from my eyes, down my face, soaking my shirt. As if all the tears I held inside these many years are finally breaking free. And I'm alone, all alone, and I have a gun and it's in my mouth, and it tastes horrible, bitter and oily and acrid all at once, and I want so badly to pull the trigger, to end it all... But I'm afraid. And the word Coward comes to mind again and I feel my Giant roar and I shake it off and I start to squeeze the trigger and the phone rings and it's my friend and she says, "Hi."

And I don't answer but I think she hears me crying because she asks, "Are you alright?"

And I still don't answer because I can't. I don't know how. The words are spinning and spinning in my head, like a hurricane of voices, lashing and raging and exploding and destroying, except they're all my voice, and it's trapped in my head and I don't know how to let it out.

And I cry, sob uncontrollably with the phone pressed against my cheek and she must have heard me because she says, "Hold on. I'm coming right over."

And she does. She comes over and she tells me it's alright but it's not alright and I cannot tell her because my voice is trapped inside. And I've hidden the gun so she won't know, so I can get it when she leaves. But I'm afraid. So afraid. But I think it will be better to end the pain once and for all. And she rocks me gently and in time my tears dry and I start to wonder if maybe it will get better someday, if I'll get better someday, if my scars will heal and my pain will lessen and let happiness back in. And I hope, a small spark deep inside, I feel it. She's brought me hope, cast a bridge across my chasm of despair. And I cling to it like my life depends on it because I think it does. And I say, "Thank you."

And she leaves and I call another friend before I can change my mind and he comes over and takes apart my gun and hides its pieces all over the house where I cannot find them. Because I ask him to, he does this, and I think he's saved my life. My life saved twice in one night, first by a phone call and compassion and then by a friend who's done my bidding without even asking why...

∞

I dream of wolves again. It's been so long since they visited me. But they're here now, tonight tearing at the fabric of my mind, eager to feast on my soul. And I almost fed it to them. But then I didn't and they are angry...so angry. And I realize that even though He isn't in my life now, He still haunts me. These are His wolves. They came with Him, why can't they leave with Him? Why won't He leave me alone, let me be?

I see Him in my dream and scream, "HAVEN'T YOU DONE ENOUGH!" And the words fly from my mouth like lightning, and in the thunderclap that follows the strangest thing happens... The wolves stop. They look at each other in confusion. They yelp and they yowl and the growl at each other, like they're discussing something. Then the wolves turn and then tear into Him, biting, shredding, clawing, ripping and He disintegrates...like a small grey rabbit, He disintegrates in my dream.

∞

I'm on the mountain now. Only a little way up the base, but it's something at least. The moon hangs heavy in the sky like an over-ripe melon, threatening to break free, smash to the ground. And it's beautiful and I shudder because I almost lost this, the beauty, the mountain, The Castle. I almost threw them all away because I almost threw my life away and now I'm glad I didn't.

The night is warm. Wind blows down the mountain, carrying scents of life and decay, the Yin-Yang of the mountain, of life and death, of hope and dread. I sigh and start to climb by moonlight, in the moonlight, like a ladder laid down by the moon, her light shows me the way. And I wonder why the moon is she and she is the moon and I find it matters naught. The moon is the moon regardless what I call her, and to me she is her and that's good, for me...

And I climb, higher and higher I climb, but the slope is gentle and my ascent is slow and I decide that for this part of my journey the path is the destination and the path is the mountain and the mountain is life and I'm alive and that is my destination, to be alive on this path now. And that is good. And I am good. And life is good. And I climb because climb I must and a smile paints my lips in the moonlight.

I throw back my head and laugh, like I haven't laughed in ages, like my life depends on it because I think it just might, I laugh. And the howling begins and a shiver of fear trails up my spine. But I shake it off and I continue climbing.

And then they appear, galloping like horses, they crest the edge of the mountain, away to my left they come, closer, closer...And I see the wolves from my dream converging, His wolves, drawing nigh. And I wonder...*Why are they here?* And, *Is this it? Is this the end?*

The wolves charge and charge, right at me, fangs bared, eyes glinting in moonlight, like agents of death with razor teeth and jaws of steel, they come...for me. But I'm not afraid, this time it's different and I don't know why. And they come closer, closer, grey lightning streaking through moonlight.

And they're so close I feel the ground rumble and I feel the heat of their breath and they leap, as one they leap... I flinch, I don't mean to but I do, and they sail over me...

And I'm alive.

They sail over me as time stretches taut and seconds stand still and I watch them. And I turn as they fly, over me, behind me, landing on... An ogre, club raised for the killing blow, was behind me... Like battering rams they pound the beast. It swings its club, connects with one wolf, smashing its life away like a bothersome insect. And the other wolves howl, so loud, so fierce, my body shudders, electrified by the sound.

And they circle the ogre and they lunge and snap and tear, always striking when it's turned away, and it turns in confusion and it's bleeding and it drops its club and falls to the ground and cries in a strange voice full of despair, "Please spare me!" and covers its head with its arms and quivers, there alone with its fear.

I wonder, can one such as this feel despair? Can a creature of evil carry seeds of goodness in its heart of hearts? Or is evil merely a name we give those we fail to understand? Certainly there is evil in the world and as I look at this creature, trembling, I realize this is different.

And the largest wolf, with dark grey fur, thick like a lion's mane, says to me. Its voice radiating power, "Oh Nameless one, we are yours to command."

I'm silent, pondering the value of life, even that of a life that would have ended mine but a moment ago. And it comes to me that I'm different too. I am neither good nor evil though my actions may be construed by others as either...depending on their beliefs and motives. All I know is that I've always done my best to be my best and often failed miserably and gotten back up and started again. Every day, my quest to be my best continues and I understand this, condemning one to die is beyond my right...

So I speak, "Why were you trying to kill me?"

The ogre moves its arm, its eyes survey me, it pushes itself up, sits, and answers, "I was sent to kill you, to stop you from discovering your true name."

I take this in, look at it, turn it over, examine it. It fits and I say, "Who sent you?"

The ogre starts to speak, stops itself, looks at the wolves all fierce teeth snarling at it, eager to snap and tear and rend, and opens its mouth again, "The Great One under the mountain." And the ogre's eyes skitter from mine like cockroaches as it looks over, down, away...into the heart of the mountain.

And I think to ask, *Why does The Great One want to stop me from discovering my true name?* But the words stop before reaching my lips because it comes to me that I know why, already inside where it matters, I know. So I leave the question alone and say instead, "Go! Leave now and never come within a day's march of me and mine again! Or my wolves will feast on your flesh..." I let the words trail off as the ogre scrambles frantically to its feet, bows and sprints away.

The wolves...my wolves, I know this to be true, they serve me, protect me now, here they do. In this place they are mine. They turn to me and bow and the grey one with fur like a lion's mane, loud enough for the fleeing ogre to hear, says, "Are you certain you don't want me to feast on that..." And he points his snout at the fleeing ogre, "tonight?" And I'm certain the wolf smiles and winks as it looks back at me.

I chuckle, "No. Not tonight." And then I remember the fallen wolf and sadness washes over me. But this sadness is appropriate because sometimes sadness is alright, at times it's healthy, even good, when it signals the end of something or spurs you to action or tells you it's time to heal but not when sadness is a burning coal clenched tightly, so tightly that it sears your soul and blackens your heart. And I know this sadness is good and it will pass...in time.

The leader, the lion-wolf, as I think of him now, says, "Let us honor the dead." And the wolves gather round their fallen friend and they howl and they howl and they howl. The sound is long and mournful and carries with it the story of the fallen wolf's life. I cannot understand the words they howl but I feel them and I see them, pictures of the fallen wolf's life hanging in the air like a tapestry of honor and courage and hope.

When the fallen wolf's story is told, to the pack, to the wind, to the world... The wolves start digging and they dig and they dig, long into the night, until morning's light crests the horizon. And when the hole is deep enough the wolves nudge their fallen friend's body into the hole and then they cover him and then they sleep and I sleep...

11

I'm sad…again, always sad, despair driving nails in the lid of my coffin…One by one by one they go, in deep, into the wood. And this sadness isn't a good sadness and I know it and I don't care because it's my sadness, the one thing no one can ever take from me.

There's something else, another thing no one can ever take from me but I've forgotten what it is and I know that's part of the problem. If I could remember what I've forgotten, the other thing that no one can take from me, I know I'd feel better but I don't care because this sadness is mine, and I wallow in it like a pig in the mud. I take my sadness and rub it all over me with thoughts and with music dragging me down…an endless bio-feedback loop of brain chemistry fueled by sadness building to a crescendo of despair, diving deeper and deeper until I'm so low that Hell is above me and Heaven a distant dream…And deeper, ever deeper still.

I just want to be loved! Why can't they see that, feel it, hear it? Why do they leave me alone? Can't they see my pain, building, building inside like an atom bomb exploding and trapped and building, searing my soul with fallout of loneliness and despair, burning my heart to ashes from which no Phoenix ever will rise?

And I grab my head to hold it together and I scream, like a caged animal, full of agony and rage and loneliness and despair, because I am caged, caught within the prison of my mind, the only prison from which I can never escape, from which I'll never escape because I've forgotten the other thing that they can never take from me and I don't know how to find it.

And the bottle slips from my fingers but fails to shatter on the ground and I reach up and grab the back of my head and slam my face into my knee, again and again and again, beating myself like He used to, punishing myself because there's no one else around to do it...

I feel warmth against my cheek and one side of my body and cold against the rest. I open my eyes and find I've been sleeping, on the mountain, with the wolves, and the lion-wolf is curled against me, keeping me warm, protecting me but not from me because no one can protect me from that. And I sit and stretch and my head hurts and I examine my nose but find it intact. No blood. I expected blood and I'm disappointed. I shrug.

And lion-wolf looks at me and says, "You were dreaming." It sounds like an accusation but I ignore it because he is my wolf and he's protecting me and perhaps the accusation is in my mind with the rest of the madness, my madness and I feel like I'm slipping again, slipping deeper and deeper, despair clawing at the edges of my mind, but I cannot slip here, this is my safe place, my escape. I won't allow it. And somehow I stop...my slide into madness.

Then I realize what lion-wolf said, it hits me hard and fast like a kick in the gut, I've been dreaming... But how..? How can I dream here if here is the dream? And if here is the dream and I've been dreaming, is there a dream too, from another place, a dream from which I cannot wake? The thought amuses me and I laugh.

Lion-Wolf scowls, stands, shakes his coat the way dogs shake off water. But it's not water that flies from his fur, its dust and dirt and pieces of mountain and I choke and cough and pound my chest to clear it. And he snorts and I swear he smiles again in the way only a wolf can smile. And I laugh harder, holding my sides, falling to the ground, and rolling around until I can hardly breathe, laughter.

But then I remember that I'm supposed to be depressed and I start examining all my reason to feel depressed again and I start sliding, sliding, sliding, and my depression grows, and grows... The more I look at them, my reasons, the things wrong in my life, the deeper my depression grows...

But then the strangest thing happens and I think, *I'm tired of feeling depressed!* And I do something about it, something that makes it less and less. I think of things I'm grateful for, I start listing them one by one by one, and my depression starts lifting. I ask myself what good can come from the challenges in my life and an answer springs to mind, *Your challenges make you stronger...*

And I remember my Giant and how strong it is and how it grew, and grew the more I realized how strong I am. And the thing I couldn't remember comes back to me. Everything is choice and no one can ever take my choices away from me. And I realize something new...

I can choose how I feel by choosing my thoughts, the thoughts I keep create my emotions, my emotions create more thoughts and those thoughts create more emotions. When I'm, unhappy in life I only need change my thoughts. And I smile and laugh and it feels good.

Lion-Wolf barks and the other wolfs gather round. "We must make haste." He growls at them, then looking at me he says, "Time is wasting. Climb on my back and let us away." And I do, I climb up and curl my fingers in his fur. Once he feels I'm secure, he gallops up the mountain and the pack follow close behind and I'm free. I'm free at last...

12

I'm in the counselor's office, my counselor, I've been visiting him every week for a while... And he's a nice enough guy but he doesn't seem to know what to say and I wonder if he believes me or if he cares or if I'm just another paycheck... And I wonder what he tells Father because they are friends and I don't trust him so I tell him just enough to get by. And he tells me that people who are abused as children grow up to be abusers, like it's a fact, written in the stone of ages. And I believe him because he's an adult and he's a counselor and he knows what he's talking about...because that's how it works, Right?

And I'm devastated because the last thing I want is to grow up and hurt others the way I've been hurt and my counselor just told me this, matter of fact, like I've no choice, no say, like I'm doomed. Might as well hang it up now because you'll never escape. And my world tilts off kilter, its axis warped now, and I don't know what to do because my mission is to help others to help them live better lives and how can I do that if I'm cursed to repeat the sins of...of...of Him?

∞

I'm back on the mountain and we're crossing a narrow cliff ledge single file. A sheer face of granite pushes on our left and a deadly drop waits on our right and it is the only way, the only path up the mountain, so we brave it. Lion-Wolf leads the way. I hold his tail like a life line and he lets me, which is something because wolves never let you touch their tails but he does, let me touch it and I hold on. And it's snowing, wind howling, darkness creeping in as the suns sinks toward the horizon and kisses the moon goodnight.

And we're half way up the mountain and I shudder to think of the rest of the journey up, up, up to the clouds and past the clouds and through them to the bitter sunlight and howling wind above. And my head spins as I walk, so carefully along the ledge, with thoughts of destiny and fate and other things equally dark. I use my tricks, the things I've learned to lift me up, to fill me with hope, but they offer only brief respite from my counselor's words marching relentlessly round my mind.

Chapter 12

I want to be better than Him! I scream in my mind, *I am better than Him!* And the ledge crumbles under my foot as if the mountain says, "Prove it!"

I scream and I slip and I fall from the ledge. And my fingers rip from Lion-Wolf's tail. And this moment of time becomes a drop of amber dripping slowly through the fabric of the cosmos, as I fall...

13

e're all at the table, Brother, Father, his wife, and I. All of us sitting at the glass table, having a discussion at father's wife's favorite table. And discussion means Brother and I are in trouble because we've done something again. And I want to speak, to defend myself, but I don't know how. My jaw works, muscles twitch, teeth grind, as the maelstrom of words and feeling swirl inside me but there's a disconnect...I can't make the words come out of my mouth because...because...

Because He used to beat me when I talked back and anything I said when He was angry was talking back and He trained me oh so well...and so I sit here silent outside and raging inside because I cannot speak, I want to speak, to tell them what really happened but I...I...I can't. My mouth refuses to open, like a stubborn mule it will not budge, so I sit at the glass table, a small child inside but nearly an adult on the outside, and listen to

Father and his wife tell me all the things Brother and I do wrong. And I take it, and take it, and take it, in silence...on the outside.

And father's wife is angry, oh so angry. Father sits there like an impotent figurehead, trying to mediate, unwilling to back her fully, unwilling to stand up for Brother or me... And that only makes her angrier. And I think Father is like a stallion someone gelded and broke. I wonder when it happened, was it the day he sent me back, to...to Mother and Him? But Father's wife cannot see his turmoil because she refuses to look past herself, or she doesn't know how, and she thinks my silence is insolence and brother is trying to defend me and that just makes it worse...

Father's wife is stuck in a feedback loop, she's looping anger like I'm looping silence and fear, and she's so, so angry, I've never seen her this angry before...And she picks up the table, the glass table, her favorite table, and smashes it against its base in an explosion of razor shards. And the color drains from her face as she realizes what she's done and I think, that anger is a is a poor master. It lies to us, tells us it'll make things better, but it never does...it never does, not this kind of anger, not the anger that destroys hearts and relationships and lives. No, this anger is a poor master indeed, one that none should ever serve...

∞

Time slows as I'm falling...falling...falling deeper and deeper down I go, down the mountain, into the abyss. But slowly, so slowly. And from the ledge, on the cliff my wolves look down, down helpless to stop my fall, to save me. And time is slow, so very slow as they grow farther and farther distant.

And I wonder as I watch the cliff rush by, what brought me here, to this place where time and space and death collide as I fall, deeper, deeper, deeper into the abyss. And my heart is filled with thoughts of things that could have been or could still be or maybe are in another time and place where I've lived a different life and walked another path. But this is my path, marred as it is with pain, scarred by ghosts of Him, haunted by thoughts of what could have been...it is my path and I am who I am because of it.

Then a realization strikes my soul like a thunderclap in the stillness of death, falling, falling, falling... And I realize that I am who I am, not because of my path but because of what I've done with my path. The path hasn't made me, my choices have made me. My path has shaped my choices, influenced them, but they are still mine. The one thing that no one can ever take from me, my power of choice. And I know this in my heart, in my bones, in my soul, in my skin, in every cell and fiber and electron and cosmic particle that makes me. I know the truth now, I could walk any path and still be who I am or walk this path, my path, and be someone completely different...because I choose, with every breath, every thought, every beat of my heart I choose to be me. And no one can ever take that away from me as I fall, down, down, down...

And time slows, slows more, stops. I hang suspended in space, a prisoner of the moment, death below me freedom above me, helpless I hang as I fall and time stands still.

And then time ticks, once. Lion-Wolf crouches.

Time ticks again. Lion-Wolf gathers himself.

Time ticks a third... Lion-Wolf's muscles bunch, like powerful springs.

Time ticks a fourth... Lion-Wolf leaps from the ledge.

Time ticks a fifth... Lion-Wolf shoots, straight at me, like an arrow of salvation.

Time ticks a sixth... Lion-Wolf overtakes me and time resumes. Wind howls past me, Lion-Wolf grasps my shoulder in his teeth. It hurts, blood flows, and I grimace. With a mighty shake, Lion-Wolf throws me sideways, throws me to a ledge lower down, a ledge I hadn't seen. And I land in a heap against the mountain...alive and I realize what he's done and I scream, "Nooooo..!"

I look over the edge and see Lion-Wolf falling, tumbling like a lost toy, down, ever deeper down into the abyss. And I know he's saved me and I'm grateful to be alive and I feel guilty that he sacrificed himself for me and I shout, "WHY?"

And he looks at me as he's tumbling, falling, falling, down, deeper down, farther down and he yells back, "You must survive!" And he vanishes from sight, into the mist, and he is...gone. And I weep...

14

I'm sitting on the couch, looking at the phone, waiting for Mother to call. And she doesn't...call. She hasn't called in nearly a year, hasn't answered when I call, I'm banished from her life, exiled because I upset her by telling her the truth, a truth she didn't want to hear, a truth I knew she didn't want to hear and I told her because I was angry and tired, tired of the questions, tired of lying to protect her from the truth. So I told her the truth and now Mother is gone from my life.

And I wonder how it is to turn off your love like that, to turn it off and cast someone you love out of your life because they hurt you. I decide I'd rather not know what that's like because knowing that might break me. As if I need more breaking.

So I sit and wait and hope that someday soon the phone will ring and it will be Mother and she will love me again, love me enough to call me, love me enough to forgive me for hurting her. And even as I think this

I know that I cannot hurt her any more than she can hurt me because she must choose to feel hurt, she must choose that meaning as I must choose my meanings. And if the power of choice is the one thing that no one can ever take away from me then it is also the one thing no one can ever take from her. And for some reason that hurts more, my choice to hurt more from the realization that Mother is choosing her hurt over her love for me.

And still I wait, wait for the phone to ring, wait for Mother to love me again...

∞

I'm on the ledge, the ledge where Lion-Wolf threw me to save my life...And I'm contemplating the meaning of life and sacrifice and pain. I thought I was safe here, safe from losing loved ones, safe from that kind of pain. I was wrong... And I think of the wonderful times I experienced with Lion-Wolf in the short time I knew him and I decide now to remember him by honoring the good he did, by remembering the good in him, good that made it impossible for him to do anything but sacrifice himself for me. Yes. I'll remember by forgetting, forgetting the sadness of his death and recalling the glory that is and always will be Lion-Wolf.

Above me my wolves howl and they howl and they howl, their voices powerful as one, harmonizing, overpowering the wind as they sing the song of Lion-Wolf, as they sing the story of his life to the pack, to the wind, to the world... And when they're finished telling the tale of Lion-Wolf, when they're done honoring him, they turn to look at me and howl again in angst and frustration. And I say to them, scream so they hear me over the wind, "Be still my friends." And they are, my wolves are still as I go inside, deep inside myself and meditate on my current situation.

And I go deeper, and deeper, and deeper until my body tingles, and fades, and drifts away and my mind calms and my thoughts flow and peace fills my soul. And I wonder at the peace, I've just lost Lion-Wolf and I feel him still, an anchor to all that is good in life, in me and I know he'll always be here for me...when I need him, here in the unknown corners of my mind where I now so carelessly wander.

I wander into relaxation, I wander into peace, I wander into the depths of my soul and the stillness between my thoughts, the gap, the void in existence from which all creation flows. And I feel the whole of my life, completed within me, now whole, and the whole of my life, now completed that is yet to come and the being which is 'I' which is 'Nameless' which is also The Unknown... The being that I Am that is Energy and Light and Hope and Goodness and me, this being wakes and wonders where its body is because I am deeper, deeper into relaxation, deeper into myself than I've journeyed before and

I've no body because I am energy, pure as the cosmos is ancient, drifting through the sands of time that are planets, suns, molecules in the universe that is I Am. And I realize that I Am Energy and I Am Light and I Am Hope and I Am Goodness and I Am Creation and Creation is me, is me and is in me and flows from me like sands of time in my universe. And then it fades and I fade and my body slowly returns...

And I wake on the ledge with my wolves howling above me in the wind and I feel energy radiating from me, bursting from my veins and I know what I must do.

To my wolves, I call, "Leave me now my friends. I'll find you on the other side." And I turn away without looking at them or waiting to see what they do. I touch the mountain face, run my hands over its coldness, its hardness presses back against my flesh and I close my eyes and feel the truth of the mountain and the truth sets me free when I feel the mark that I knew I'd find and I press it hard, shoving against the immovable might of the mountain, and it moves, an inch, and I open my eyes and the mountain moves a foot as I press, an ant moving a mountain, I Am.

But the mountain isn't moving. It's a door, swinging open silently into darkness and lightning splits the sky behind me, pulsing for a beat, throbbing with energy as the sky caresses the earth with its power, lighting the darkness like a flash strobe and a tunnel lies before me, sloping down, curving deep, out of sight, into blackness. It is my path and I must take it. I know this as certainly as I know I Am. So I step inside, into the great blackness, and I take three steps and the door slams shut behind me... And I am in the mountain, in the great blackness, as unforgiving as time, as oppressive as hate, and as necessary to me as my light.

I take another step into the great unknown of the mountain... And I shiver because I Am alone...

15

'm dreaming. I know I'm dreaming because I'm younger again and I'm still living with Mother and with...with Him. And I'm stuck in the dream and I cannot wake but I want to wake because I know what's coming, which is sometimes worse than not knowing what's coming, and this is one of those times... when knowing is worse, much worse.

And I'm in an elevator with Brother and we were playing around and we got the elevator stuck between floors and the alarm is going off and the doors are open on the inside, which is never supposed to happen when they're closed on the outside. But it has and the alarm is going off...

And He is angry. I hear Him yelling at us and I quake like a sapling in a hurricane right before it rips from the ground, just like that, I shiver and quake.

They get the doors open somehow. I don't remember how and in the dream it doesn't matter, but now they are open and Brother and I are standing outside the broken elevator and He is angry. So very angry. His face is red and He's shaking and veins bulge on His forehead, pulse in time with his raging heart, and the other man there, the one who got us out, is telling Him it's really okay... But it's not okay, not for Him because we embarrassed Him, brother and I did. And that is an unforgivable sin...

And the other man leaves and He grabs us by the back of our necks, lifting us like we're naughty kittens. But it's not our mittens we've lost it's His pride and that is worse, so...much...worse... And we get to the car and he throws us inside and the dream ends because the memory ends and there's nothing for days after that, just blankness, and emptiness, and faded ghosts of pain...

∞

I work my way down the tunnel, cautiously, trailing my fingers against the rough-hewn stone of the wall, stepping slowly, keeping my weight on my back foot until I'm certain the tunnel floor is there. I repeat this process again and again. Keep to the wall, feel for the floor, transfer my weight to my front foot. Over and over and over. It's slow moving, mind numbing, down, down into the darkness...deeper and deeper into the heart of the mountain I go.

My mind plays tricks on me. I imagine lightening of the tunnel ahead, something to break the monotony of blackness, and then I blink and it's gone. Replaced by what was always there, black so pitch that light may never have existed. And it doesn't matter how long I wait, my eyes cannot adjust to this because there's no light, not even a sliver. And I travel down, down, deeper, ever so slowly, deeper into this realm that light forgot.

I hear voices, whispering sounds full of malice and despair, all around me, circling me, taunting me. And with my other hand I lash out, in the black I swing with power fueled by all the anger inside me...but nothing's there and I realize the voices are in my head, they are my voices, haunting me. And I make a choice, I use my power and ignore them. And I fill my mind with happy thoughts and I'm surprised to find I have them, happy thoughts of happy times mingled with sadness and I realize that the more I search, the more happiness I find because Joy is in me, deep down in my heart, like I'm deep in the mountain's heart. And I realize that as I seek I shall find. The more I seek despair the more there is in me and the more I seek happiness the more there is in me. And I choose happiness, in this, unlikely place, deep, deep down in the dark happiness finds me because I let it.

And I go deeper and deeper into the mountain and time seems to stop, like the grains of sand in the hourglass of my life are frozen in mid-flight. They cannot go down with me and they cannot go up without me so they are frozen here, an eternal now, waiting for me in this place.

My mind drifts, the mechanical functions of feeling the wall and feeling for safe footing continue managed by my unconscious mind, and my consciousness, released of this charge, takes flight deep into my past, into the heart of my past, like the heart of the mountain, deeply my mind goes. And I relive painful events from another perspective, an observer of my life instead of a participant, and I find they hurt less and so I choose to keep them this way, detached because this is my power... To choose to also learn what I need to, so the events are never repeated on me or by me or with me, I release my mind to learn what it must so the cycles are broken and keep these learnings safe because the cycles are broken as it releases the pain. And with the release comes peace so profound it's like floating through the stars in a cocoon of light, safe, warm, silent, at zero because after all I am stardust encased in flesh, stardust that is flesh, and I smile. Here, deep in the dark under the heart of the mountain I smile because I Am Joy and Joy is me and Life is what I choose...

16

Father and his wife have moved out, they built a home thirty miles away and decided to live there and they gave me the choice to live in the old house by myself, alone to finish my senior year of high school, alone, and I chose to stay in the old house... alone. And it's mostly okay but often is lonely and I miss Brother because he's in the army now, so far away and Mother has never come to visit. I've seen her once in the past five years and I talk to Mother rarely but I do talk to her. She finally called and then acted like she'd never disowned me or disavowed me or threw me out with the emotional trash...and I tell myself I don't care but I know I do and mostly I'm okay...

And I see Father once every two weeks or so, which really isn't that different from when he lived here because he was always gone, physically gone or emotionally gone, he was both. And it really doesn't matter which it is because gone is gone...and I feel like an inconvenience to him, like a biology experiment gone awry... Especially since Mother told me that Father never wanted children... And I believe her. But he has children and so he's endured it, after a fashion, he endures.

As I sit on the couch I stare out the window, sunlight shining on the neighbor's brick wall. And I wonder if sunlight can shine on brick but decide it doesn't matter because these are my thoughts and I have the power to choose and I do. I choose sunlight shining on bricks because it feels better. And I like choosing to feel better Now that I know this is my power. It holds the darkness at bay.

And I miss Brother and talk to him occasionally and he says he's okay but I can hear the lies in his voice because I know him and we learned to lie when we were young to protect each other. And the sound of a lie is the same from youth to adulthood, lies ring false, and his words ring false when he says he's okay because I know the Army is full of bullies and Brother has been troubled by bullies all his life, starting with Him, the biggest bully of all. And I think it's interesting that even though He's been gone from our lives for years now, Brother placed himself in the Army where many others so easily channel the spirit of Him...

∞

I see light ahead, the faintest glow, pulsing like a heartbeat, and I blink, expecting it to vanish like all the times before but it doesn't. And it's hot, so hot here under the mountain as I journey to the heart of it. I've traveled and slept and traveled and slept until I feel like the character in the famous book about the ring, the one who lives under the mountain with the ogres... Except I'm sane, at least I think I Am and there's no one here to tell me different, so it's decided...I'm sane. And the only precious thing I have with me is my power to choose and I use it constantly because every moment, every breath, every thought is choice, and I've had it all my life even though I didn't always know it. And if I've had this power all my life then that means I got it on my birthday, the day I was born, and I guess there's that similarity too. But I am sane and I'm human, and I haven't ever eaten ogre, so I choose another line of thought because that's my power, to choose.

I continue walking down, down, deeper down and the light in the tunnel gets brighter and brighter until it stings my eyes. And I blink away the tears but not the burning because it's been so long since I've seen the light. But see it I do and I rejoice to bask in the brilliance here, in the heart of the mountain.

The tunnel ends in a colossal room. Light, brighter than the noon-day sun, radiates from a pulsing source at its center, paints the walls with golden hues but is lost before reaching the ceiling. I leave the safety of the tunnel and walk toward the light where I know my answer awaits...

17

$\mathcal{I}$n the stillness of the night my eyes grow heavy and sleep finds me, takes me into its arms and carries me away. And I find myself standing in a hallway, in the old house. Standing there in shock and pain. Father is acting like...like...like Him. Father's angry with Brother, over what I've no idea. Father was chasing Brother through the house, chasing Brother like he was going to hurt him, punish him, make him pay... All phrases I've heard before but never from the mouth or actions of Father.

And then I remember, I have seen this Father before, when I was only a little child, when he and Mother were still married I accidentally walked in on them... And he was so angry, enraged at my innocent interruption that he lifted me up and slammed me against the wall, his forearm at my throat, choking me, my tiny feet dangling high on the wall and I couldn't breathe and Mother had to pry his arm from my throat because he was choking me and I couldn't breathe and I was turning blue and Mother saved me from Father... So, yes I've seen this side of him before and I hate it.

And Brother is scared and I don't know what I'm doing because Brother is older and should be protecting me but I throw myself between Brother and Father and say, "I know you're stronger than me and I know you can kill me if you want because of your training but you're not hurting Brother without going through me!"

And I can't believe I said the words but say them I did. And I stand there shaking, afraid for my life and unwilling to let Father hurt Brother without going through me first, for whatever that's worth. But it turns out it's worth a lot because Father's face seems to melt, like all the rage drains from it, and he looks like a lost little boy and he shakes his head and mumbles something that I can't understand and he turns and shuffles away...

∞

The light is growing nearer, here in the heart of the mountain, pulsing like the beating of a heart, the mountain's heart, in time with my heart the light pulses as I walk toward it. And my side explodes with pain like a thousand knives cutting me, piercing me, slashing me to pieces. And my body seems to collapse, then lifts from the ground, flies across the room, and smashes into the wall. More pain, filling me with agony like I never knew existed, which is saying something, and I slide down the wall and crumple in a heap on the floor.

"I knew you'd come." A voice like sandpaper over glass grates the words.

I cough, blood coats my lips, splatters the floor. I look up. A man, largest I've ever seen that wasn't a giant, with legs like barrels and arms like tree trunks and a chest the size of a small car, looms over me smashing a war-hammer, the size of an anvil, against his palm. *How am I alive?* I wonder. *He should have killed me with one blow.* The man's face is lost in shadows, covered by a cowl where I cannot see it. But I know who this is. The Great One Under The Mountain.

And I find myself saying, "You don't seem so great to me..." And I think, *that was stupid.* But I said it and he heard it and now I'm going to pay. And I cough again, and pink mist sprays from my lips.

He roars, a sound like an enraged animal, which suits him. And he raises the hammer he smashed me with and swings it again...

18

I'm dreaming still but the dream's changed and now I'm in the upstairs living room...with a friend. *But is he a friend?* I wonder because a friend wouldn't do the things he's done, things to make me angry and to hurt me and to see how far he can exert control over my emotions, the control that I give him by choosing to react instead of respond. But it's control nonetheless and I give it and he takes it.

And he's screaming at me, my friend, screaming that I'm no good and that I'm a failure and that I'm worthless and of all the daggers he's thrown at me, that one hurts the most because a friend would never say something like that, would never say something that cuts so deep... Right?

I'm raging inside, all thoughts cease because I'm pure emotion and the emotion is rage and rage is me and the world goes red and I hear the ghost of Him urging me on...chanting, "Hit him! Hit him! Make him pay!" And I feel my arm draw back, like a bow before the arrow flies, my arm is ready to launch and my fist is tight and the hate burns like a bright bonfire raging so hot inside.

And from the depths of my soul a voice screams *STOP! If you hit him you'll never stop!*

I know the voice is right because I see a vison of me pounding and pounding and pounding relentlessly on my friend, who isn't my friend because he's become the avatar of everything that's ever hurt me. Pounding, as if every blow will erase the pain but doesn't because hurting others never heals us and is wrong and he deserves better.

And I want to stop but the anger and the pain and the hurt, a lifetime of hurt exploding in this moment, is too great, my walls are crumbling and I cannot contain it... And the voice inside, realizing I cannot stop this tsunami of rage and hurt and pain, says, *Then hurt yourself instead...*

And I do. I lash out, punch the window next to me, because it's the nearest thing. But the window fights back. It shatters and slices and cuts my flesh, flesh so fragile that the illusion of immortality bright in youth flees like a frightened grey rabbit running from a gun. And the window bites deep, its teeth searing skin and muscle and tendons and nerves and finally biting bone... But the bones in my arm stop it and I pull my arm out of the window in shock and my heart beats and blood flies from my arm and paints the opposite wall in the room like a surrealist piece of abstract art...

∞

The war-hammer falls like a death sentence toward my upturned face. And time gifts me a moment, this moment, once again suspended like a drop of amber falling through the cosmos...time stands still. And the war-hammer stops and the Great One Under The Mountain is frozen, his muscles bunched and frozen with kinetic energy. And it comes to me that I'm dying already. The blow I took, blindsided by the Great One, is fatal. And I laugh because the Great One has no honor. I realize that some are great because they earn it by helping others and making the world a better place and some are great because of fear, which isn't greatness in the end. Great One is a hollow title when bestowed in terror. And this Great One is the hollow kind because in his heart of hearts he is a coward who rules with fear or he would have faced me from the start.

And without knowing why, I close my eyes and go deep inside...Deeper and deeper I go, deeper down, down into the abyss of my psyche, ever deeper until I find the place where thoughts stand still and reality bends and I see my highest self floating like a cloud of stardust in the depths of my soul, of my mind, the depths of me. And my highest self asks, in a voice that is mine but isn't mine because it radiates wisdom, wisdom born before the dawn of time, wisdom from the great mind that binds us all, it asks, "Why?"

And I know why is the question that holds all questions within it and why gives me the power to say, "Heal me." And I know I'm ready to live, to truly live, to cast aside the chains that bind me, the chains so carefully placed by pain and hate and hurt and hopelessness, the chains I've worn my entire life... But now, now I'm ready to shatter the chains and live! And I cannot live when my body is dying so I say again, "Heal me!"

My highest self simply nods and a vision of my perfect body appears before me, floating beside my highest self, it appears and I know it's the blueprint, the perfect blueprint of my body. And my highest self reaches in and pulls the plans for the damaged sections of my body and hands them to me and says, "Integrate."

And I do. I close my eyes within me, deep within the heart of me I find I've eyes to close as well, I Am me within me, the whole self within the self that I Am...and I close them and envision my perfect body blueprint integrating with my body NOW and the Healing Begins.

And then nothing for a time because the integration continues as time stands still and the war-hammer waits above me, poised for the killing blow...

19

*A*nd the dream continues but it's not a dream it's a memory and it's a dream because it happened once and I'm dreaming it now. And I'm lying on the table in the operating room and the surgeons are wrapping my arm in a tourniquet because they can't put me under and they try to squeeze the blood out of my arm before tightening the tourniquet but they hit the nerve, exposed, raw, lightning flashes up my arm, lifting me off the table. And they cannot operate if I'm thrashing around but they have to operate to save my arm... so they decide to leave the blood and tighten the tourniquet...

Then they fill my arm with something to deaden the pain. And it does mostly, but I can still feel everything above the tourniquet and some things below but it's the best they can do and I have no choice but to endure it.

Time stretches again, endless agony, endless confusion, consciousness phasing in and out like a flickering light. And I endure. I endure until they say they're finished and they remove the tourniquet and they give me something and blackness takes me in its warm embrace...

∞

Integration continues as the war-hammer looms, threatening death as reward for my healing. But I cannot concern myself with that now. I feel muscles heal and capillaries grow and bones knit together as the integration of my perfect body blueprint into my body continues and the Healing Continues NOW!

And my consciousness drifts, a ship lost at sea, lost in the sea of the cosmos, the sea of awareness, the sea of I Am, as the Healing Continues NOW and wholeness is carefully, perfectly restored.

I see a vison in my vison of the world as it will be when humanity learns the thing that no one can ever take away from you, the power of choice, the power to give meaning, the power to live every moment as a gift because every moment is a gift of Now. And the world unfolds before me like a spring rose and the sweet smell of peace and harmony and love for others, love for all, wafts across the fabric of time and I realize that the time is Now because all time is Now and Now is forever unfolding like the rose. And if I cannot see the time it's merely because that point has yet to pass my awareness.

And I feel a shift and my lungs fill with air and the pain is gone because my body is restored. I lunge to the side as the war-hammer crashes down, down like a war-head where my head was a moment ago. Bits of rock and metal fly, shrapnel from the impact, they cut my back and pepper my skin with drops of blood. But now I know. And I let my perfect body blueprint restore me and the cuts heal and the pain fades as I roll quickly away.

The Great One looks at the place where my head was but a moment ago. His face bunches up like he's tasted something especially foul and he roars and he roars and he roars again. This time his rage shakes the mountain. He looks for me, swiveling his head as far as it goes in both directions until he finds me. But I'm not hiding, I'm not sure why, I should hide, from him, from his hate, from his brutality, but I don't.

No...I don't hide. Instead I discover words leaping from my mouth as I stand tall and proud to face him, "You don't seem so great to me..." And I smile as he charges me...

20

The dream, the memory, blended in a reality that exists wholly within my mind, continues because reality is as I see it, feel it, hear it, think it, reality is a construct of all these things bound with the elusive glue of time. Time drifts and I'm sitting in my room with my arm in a sling and my head in my good hand which isn't my good hand because my good hand is the one the window chewed up and spit out in a fit of malice and glee that was born within me and manifested in shattered glass. And I'm having to learn to do everything with my other hand and it's difficult and I'm feeling sorry for myself and I know that's as productive as it sounds, which is to say, not at all...

And a memory comes to me, within the memory that is my dream, of a time long past when I was only three. I walk with Mother through the grass in the field outside our trailer home and the sun shines brightly down and the wind caresses my cheek and tousles my hair and we're making a game of jumping over dried out cow-pies, Mother and I play the game and I laugh and I laugh and my heart is full of love and it's wonderful.

And I'm in mid-step, ready to jump when Mother grabs my coat and snatches me back, lifting me from the ground. And she's holding me and crying and I don't know what's going on because we were playing a game and having fun and now Mother's crying and I think it's my fault. But she sees this and she wipes her tears and says, "No. You're okay. But look..." And she points. And I look and realize, even in my three year old mind, that the cow-pie I almost leapt over was in truth a sleeping rattlesnake and even my three year old mind knows that rattlesnakes kill...

So I hug Mother back and we go home and everything is good and I know that she will always protect me...my three year old self knows this. Knows it and feels betrayed by the truth of what will be.

But in my memory within my dream I talk to my three year old self. I tell my younger self that everything will be alright in the end and that Mother is doing the best she knows how and that things will get tough, but I'm tougher and stronger than the things that happen to me. And then I tell my younger self the secret that I wish someone had told me at that age. I tell it about the thing that no one can ever take away from me, the power to choose, to choose my meaning, to choose my path, that every moment, every breath, every heartbeat, every second of life blossoms with choice and that knowing this allows me to choose my life.

And my three year old self looks at me with a puzzled frown and then smiles and says, "Okay." And goes chasing after Mother. I hope my younger self remembers and through remembering someday understands. And I feel a shift inside and I know that my younger self does and did and will remember and when the time is right will understand.

And I smile as I fade from the dream or the dream fades from me...

$$\infty$$

I dodge the Great One's charge, feint to the left, pause a beat then dive to the right as his war-hammer comes crashing down. He's committed to the blow, like a one trick pony or a rampaging bull, he can't stop until he's done, not until the war-hammer slams home. I use this time, as the hammer falls, to land a side-kick on the outside edge of his kneecap. A kick that should have snapped his knee... Instead my foot bounces off, ineffective. He's too big, I'm not even sure he felt it... So I roll again, confusing him, and come up standing closer to the pulsing light at the center of the heart of the mountain, the light that is the heart itself. He sees me, screams, charges. I dive away at the last moment and we both reset. But now I'm farther away from the heart and he knows it and I imagine a smile creeping across his face but can't see it for the cowl he hides beneath.

"You cannot keep this up forever, nameless one." The Great One snarls and tightens his hands on the haft of the war-hammer, twisting them back and forth over the metal, making it groan.

"Neither can you." I reply stepping closer to the heart. He lunges. I dodge. He charges. I dance away, landing a solid hook to his kidney as I pass by. He doesn't even flinch. We're like the mongoose and the grizzly, the two of us. He's all raw strength and power and I'm all speed but he can't strike me and my blows seem useless... So we continue, each waiting for the other to tire, for our chance.

And then chance favors me as I change tack. If I can't hurt his bones or organs, perhaps I can use his nerves against him.

I set him up by sprinting toward the heart of the mountain. He obliges by leaping to block my path. This time as the war-hammer swings I dodge the head, the haft, his arm and then land a penetrating blow in the nerve cluster on the inside of his arm, between his biceps and triceps I slam my fist, knuckles biting deep in the nerves, with all my might. Then I dart to safety.

He roars again but his arm is stunned, useless for now, and the hammer falls to the ground with a resounding thud as his arm hangs...dead at his side. For now. And he seems confused, like this is the first time any foe has hurt him, ever.

And I smile and sprint for the heart of the mountain. Racing past his dead arm. And I'm closing in and I know I only have to touch it, touch the heart and my name will be restored and the knowledge will come and whatever else the Great One fears will be fulfilled, here in the heart of the mountain.

I'm close, so close now. The Great One screams and rages and bellows behind me. And I see the heart, it's an orb, the size of a human head, floating, a star among strands of light, like the fabric of the universe and time combined and gave birth to it here, under the heart of the mountain. I stop running and approach slowly because that seems the right thing to do. And I reach out my fingertips and emotional chaos swirls inside me and I reach closer and closer and time explodes as my life expands all around me, and my fingertips are nearly there, close enough to brush it. But not yet. Not yet.

And something slams into me from behind and I think my fingertips brush the heart but I can't be sure because everything goes black...

21

*A*nd I'm sitting alone in the house that Father and his wife bought, the house that they left me in, alone because they moved away, alone because Brother is in the Army, alone because I'm afraid to let anyone in. My walls are too high, too think, too strong to ever let others in. So I wander through life, a stranger in my skin, presenting a facade to everyone I meet. My friends don't know me, not the real me. They don't see the darkness boiling beneath the surface, they don't see the pain that defines me. That I've let define me because I've forgotten again the one thing that no one can ever take away from me and I know I've forgotten it and I'm trying to care enough to find it...

But I turn on the music and wallow in my thoughts and spiral down, down, down into despair, to the place where I'm comfortably numb but that's a lie because the numbness isn't, it's pain dialed so high that it short-circuits my brain like static, so loud it drowns out everything else while making you deaf in the process. And it's still there, the pain is still there and the darkness is still there and the despair is deep in me.

And in my despair I wander like a lost child in a desert, dying from thirst, because I keep forgetting the one thing they can never take away from me. The one thing I keep giving away and loosing and fighting for again. And a voice in the back of my mind asks, *Wouldn't it be better to stop giving it away?*

And I know the answer is, Yes! And I swear, make a solemn oath to keep it once I find it, to never let it go. But I've no idea how to get there from here and I keep putting myself here because I've never learned how to keep it when I find it and here is Hell and Hell is where I am and that's my life... So I do something I rarely do, which makes it a contradiction because I'm doing it now...but I don't care, and I drink my troubles away until the blackness swallows me...

I wake with my arms bound above me. They hurt, like the time the surgeons tightened the tourniquet on my arm, they hurt. But I stifle the scream that begs come out because I know it brings them running, and they'll come and torture me until I fade away. And darkness has become my old friend for in its warmth I find respite from pain.

So I stop the scream before it leaves me and I whimper softly instead. I Am still The Nameless, and now The Forgotten, cast within the dungeons under the heart of the mountain, deep, deep inside. I thought I touched the heart before the blackness stole me...but I was wrong, I didn't. And I still don't know my name and I've been here for so long, so very long, forgotten, thrown away like the trash life told me I Am.

But still a glimmer of hope burns within. Because I know here what I forgot there and I know someday I'll pass my knowledge back across the void, the gap, the timeless boundary that separates here from there and there from here. And all I can do is endure here, and hope here, and pray for the light to reach me there before I end it in desperation or do something unforgivable there...

And I go deep inside and ask my highest self to help repair the damage and it does, brings me the necessary sections of my perfect body blueprint so I can integrate and heal. And the healing lasts until the damage is done again and then we repeat the dance. Pain. Healing. Pain. Healing. And on and on and on...

And from time to time the Great One visits me and gloats. Oh how he gloats. He struts back and forth and flings curses at me and beats me and laughs, his vile, rasping laugh, and hate stirs with me but I forgive it before it grows because I know hate's fires are all consuming and I'm unwilling to burn. And I've seen his face and it is His face but different than His because it's all the faces of Him in the world, all the Hims, as Legion combined, the worst of Them rolled up in Legion, the face of the darkest part of Them, the parts that seem damaged beyond repair. And Legion knows of the other me and knows that keeping me here makes His influence over me stronger there and oh how He wants to see me burn.

So I bide my time and endure the pain and loneliness by exploring the depths of my mind and choosing to survive...

22

Stars shine bright above me, millions and millions of specks sparkling the sky. Headlights light my way, casting life-saving brilliance a few hundred feet at a time, they keep me safe, they keep me on track, they show the way. And it reminds me that I don't need to always know the whole journey ahead, sometimes I only need to see a few hundred feet at a time, sometimes less, only enough to know where to step or where to steer my car... I only need to see far enough to keep me alive and on the road of life.

And I'm running away, chasing the dawn, racing toward it, trying desperately to stay awake. I'm running away from my broken heart but no matter what I do it's following me...

I thought I knew love. I thought I was loved and I'm certain I do love but the problem is I can't seem to recognize love when it's offered to me. So I doubt and I question and I beg and I demand because when we can't love ourselves we never fully believe others can love us...and in the end I drive them away, those who love me, I drive them out with my fear of them leaving.

I know it's ironic. I know it and I hate it and I don't know what to do about it. So I'm doing the only logical thing and that's running away from my loss and my pain and my fears...

I lost my love and I packed my car and I fled in the night. And I've been driving two hours and I've got twelve more hours to drive and I'm so tired but I'm unwilling to stop... So I bounce down the freeway like a pinball between the yellow lines hoping I don't tilt the machine.

And my mind spins with all the scenarios I've lived with the love I lost and fabricates new ones just to keep me crazy as I drive down the freeway under the stars in the blackest night and fight to stay awake...

∞

Awake... The pain in my shoulders and wrists brings me back from the abyss. And I no longer care if I scream when I wake because the guards long ago tired of tormenting me. They know my real torture is being locked away, here under the heart of the mountain with the true heart so close, so close and infinitely far from me. But I don't scream because I no longer have the need. I simply wake, assess my state and then go inside to begin the healing, my healing, a choice that none can ever take from me, my power to access my perfect body blueprint and integrate it Now to Heal.

And when the healing's done I sigh and shake my head and wonder what delights my mind holds in store for me today. *Is it today?* Time has no meaning when day blurs to night because the sun never shines for you, down on you, and you're wasting away like a forgotten piece of flotsam, rotting in the chaos of time. And I've learned so much from exploring inside, from quieting my mind and entering the gap that I've no words to express it. But always when I come back I'm here, shackled, bound, my chains greater than my might but not greater than my spirit.

I hear the soft pad, pad, pad of footfalls coming down the hall and I wonder which guard is coming to visit me now and what special delight this guard will bring before my healing begins anew.

And the door to my cell protests as it opens, the crack and creek of metal wasted by time, but open it does and the guard comes in bearing light, a torch, and I cringe because fire takes the longest to heal...but heal it does, in time. Time. My friend, my foe, my servant, my master... time. It and my thoughts are all I have now.

And the guard creeps closer, it wears a cloak and hood, not the normal attire or behavior of my guards, no boasting, no bravado, no malice...no, just cautiously creeping forward as if afraid of what it will find. I realize that not all eyes have adjusted to the blackness in my cell and then that the guard may not be able to see me just yet. So I save it the trouble and say in jest, "Halt! Who enters my realm?"

To my surprise the guard stops and stands deathly still. And I let the silence hang there, growing larger and more uncomfortable by the moment, but not for me, silence is my friend. So I wait. And when the guard decides to break it, the silence that is, it says, "You're alive! I hoped. Oh I hoped." Which is weird because my normal guards demand a response before tossing in my food and in so doing assure themselves that I'm alive...

Then I recognize the voice and say, "Hold your torch near your face and remove your hood please..." And it does and I gasp. Before me stands the ogre I spared so long ago on the mountain side. And I say, "What brings you here Ogre?" I decide it best to refrain from reminding it of my threat to kill it should I ever lay eyes on it again. After all, I'm hardly in a place to defend myself.

The ogre steps forward, slowly, cautiously, as if afraid I'll bite, and says, "I couldn't take it anymore. I knew he captured you but I only recently discovered your whereabouts." The ogre glanced around quickly, surveying the room to make sure I'm the only one present before continuing, "After you spared my life... I knew I would never forgive myself if I left you here to rot."

I ponder this for a time, though not too long given my circumstances, and say, "I neither knew ogres could be so eloquent in speech or kind of heart. How can I trust you?" After all I remind myself, the last time I met this beast it was fully intent on killing me at the command of the Great One.

Drawing keys from its pocket, the ogre steps closer still and says, "We truly haven't time. I must free you before the guards come back." I agree and he does, unlocks the shackles from my wrists and ankles, and then helps me to my feet.

I try not to show my weakness but I am weak and we both know it. Though I've learned the art of healing I haven't the sustenance to do much else but heal, meditate, and sleep. And the ogre lifts me like a child and carries me from the room, into the hallway, and away to some unknown destination...

23

The sun brightens the horizon as I race toward it. Finally, lifesaving light, giving me new hope, as my body wakes and my mind stirs and the night fades behind me. And I drive and I drive and I drive into the sunrise because I'm running away from my broken heart.

And then I think, *What if I'm running toward my new life? What if I'm remembering my power and making the changes I must to live it?*

And then I remember the thing that no one can ever take from me but that I've so often given away...my power to choose. That every moment, precious as life itself, contains countless choices and each choice matters because every choice is a new path with a new destination, and as long as I'm aware of my choices and seek to make the world a better place, all paths are good because I am good, deep in my heart where it matters most. I Am Good. And I promise myself as I drive into the sunrise and greet this, the new day dawning on my life, that no matter what happens to me or around me or in me, from now on I'll never give away my power of choice, never!

∞

The ogre creeps silently along the passages. He seems to know when and where to hide and when and where to run. And he does both with equal ease. All the while carrying me like a child in his arms. And then after a time we come to the room with the pulsing light and it burns my eyes for I've been in shadow so long. And my eyes tear up and my face is wet and my head feels like the light is boring directly into my brain...but I endure it because this is a good pain and endure it I must if I want to ever see the sun again, or more, if I want to know my name.

And the ogre is close to the heart, creeping unnoticed, silently along, when a voice shouts, "Halt! None are allowed near the heart!"

The ogre stops, looks me in the eyes, winks and hurls me at the heart under the mountain which is the heart of the mountain. And I land atop it in a tangled heap of flesh and bone and I start to slide off but grasp it tightly, so tightly.

As I tighten my grip on the heart, a pulse of light explodes from it, like the mountain's been holding its breath, waiting for this moment and can finally exhale.

At first my fingers are weak and my arms shake and my body continues to slide. But the light gives me strength, feeding my soul, my higher self, my body, and mind, filling me with energy and light. And I know my name and it is a good name because it is mine and always has been...but circumstances and life and hatred and sorrow and agony and despair and hopelessness caused me to forget. And Now I Remember my Name and my Name fills me with Power.

And the voice that shouted for the ogre to halt is furious and he calls the alarm and I hear feet approaching heavily, quickly, like a stampede under the mountain. And then the sounds of battle rage behind me. But I keep looking at the heart, pulsing in time with my heart, of this there is no doubt, the stone throbs and strobes with every pulse of blood through my veins. And I grow stronger and stronger and stronger and I can feel my muscles twitch and throb and grow as my body grows, larger, stronger, until I'm standing on the ground, standing and holding onto the heart with a single hand. I'm eye to eye with the ogre now, my friend the ogre who's fighting off a hoard of guards.

I release the stone and smile as I enter the fray.

Imbued with light and power I Am Unstoppable. I swat the guards like flies, one, two, three, and on and on until they give up and run. But the Great One Under The Mountain doesn't give up. He saunters into the heart's chamber as if he hasn't a care in the world. But he does. Oh he does. I see it etched in the lines round his eyes, deep lines, full of fear and hate. If I'd seen sorrow there things might go differently, but I didn't so they won't.

Our eyes meet and we charge and we clash, like twin titans we battle under the mountain. And the mountain shakes and groans and the heart throbs, beating, beating in time with mine, building to a staccato as we battle on.

He is still the grizzly but I'm no longer the mongoose. I'm the cheetah, the lion, the tiger, and though he lands blows and breaks bones and sends blood flying from my various wounds, my body heals as quickly as he damages it and I disassemble him accordingly.

And he is gone, the Great One, who was never Great, is dead under the heart of the mountain and none shall mourn his passing...

I slap my friend the ogre on the back. I bow to the heart, thanking it, pledging it my service. Wherever evil lurks in this land, I'll find it. I'll root it out and deal with it appropriately. And then we leave the chamber under the mountain in search of my wolves.

I Am Hero. This is my name, my path, my honor. And I know the thing that no one can ever take from me. It is my power and I'll use it every day to *choose light* and *hope* and *love* and *joy* and I'll *make the world a bet-*

ter place. And though this chapter in my tale is finished, my journey is just beginning...

Epilogue

$\mathcal{I}$ pull into the driveway, park my car, and sink behind the wheel. Fatigue coats my mind, wiping my thoughts away like an elixir of forgetfulness, turning my fourteen hour drive into a waking dream. And I shake my head and take a deep breath, open the door, and step out of my car, each movement a sheer act of will. The afternoon sun shines on me like a bright song of happiness and I walk to the door and I knock.

Grandmother cracks open the door and she sees me and her eyes open wide and her mouth makes a small "O" of surprise and then she smiles, the smile of comfort and acceptance I remember from my youth and fatigue grants me brief respite as the warmth of love washes over me.

I smile back and say, "Hi." And wave, a small thing, like a shy child waiving at a new friend because I never warned her I was coming to visit or stay and even though

I know it's alright there's still the part of me that expects rejection from those I love.

And Grandmother smiles back and says, "Well aren't you a sight for sore eyes." And she stands back and says, "Come in." And I do because this is the first day of my new life...

I'm standing on top of The Mountain. Wind whips my hair with its cold lash and the sun sinks low on the horizon, like a giant golden compass pointing the way, my way, leading me on. And my wolves are coming. They aren't here yet but I've called them and they're coming, I feel it, and I know they'll be here soon. My friend the ogre is at my side and he's changing, different now, darkness is gone from his heart and light changes him just like light changes me because when light fills my heart darkness vanishes and it shows on the outside when you let the light in. And I have and it radiates from me now, the light does.

And I cannot see The Castle that time forgot, The Castle that knows me and is seeking me as I am seeking it, but I know it's there, in the distance and I must go to it because it's waiting for me and I'm waiting for it... though I no longer know why. But I know it's vital to me, to my evolution, to my journey, to my life and I choose to go because I have that power and the choice is mine and I choose Life and I choose Hope and I choose Honor and I choose my Power and I choose Love and I choose all the Good things that life offers me and that I offer life because I Am Life and life is me.

And my story unfolds because *I Am Hero!*

Hire Roland to Speak for Your Organization or at Your Event:

http://www.rolandbyrd.co/roland-speaks/

Roland Byrd is the author of seven personal development and transformational books, two Sci-Fi/Fantasy books, contributing author to the bestselling book *The Prosperity Factor*—with Joe Vitale, and the founder of *Life 180 University*. His passion is helping people unlock their true power, be their best selves, and master their destiny.

You Want Roland at Your Event!

Roland presents with passion, humor, and energy. He engages his audience and is easy to understand. He uses analogies, stories from his own life, and real-world examples to drive home the principles he teaches.

Book Roland for Your Event Today!
http://www.rolandbyrd.co/roland-speaks/